GOOD D🐾G

9

sweater weather

by
Cam Higgins

illustrated by
Ariel Landy

LITTLE SIMON

New York   London   Toronto   Sydney   New Delhi

LITTLE SIMON
An imprint of Simon & Schuster Children's Publishing Division
1230 Avenue of the Americas, New York, New York 10020
First Little Simon paperback edition August 2022
Copyright © 2022 by Simon & Schuster, Inc.
Also available in a Little Simon hardcover edition.
All rights reserved, including the right of reproduction in whole or in part in any form.
LITTLE SIMON is a registered trademark of Simon & Schuster, Inc., and associated colophon is a trademark of Simon & Schuster, Inc.
For information about special discounts for bulk purchases, please contact Simon & Schuster Special Sales at 1-866-506-1949 or business@simonandschuster.com.
The Simon & Schuster Speakers Bureau can bring authors to your live event. For more information or to book an event contact the Simon & Schuster Speakers Bureau at 1-866-248-3049 or visit our website at www.simonspeakers.com.
Designed by Leslie Mechanic
Manufactured in the United States of America 0722 LAK
10 9 8 7 6 5 4 3 2 1
Library of Congress Cataloging-in-Publication Data
Names: Higgins, Cam, author. | Landy, Ariel, illustrator. | Good dog ; 9.
Title: Sweater weather / by Cam Higgins ; illustrated by Ariel Landy.
Description: First Little Simon paperback edition. | New York : Little Simon, 2022.
Series: Good dog ; 9 | Audience: Ages 5–9. | Summary: The weather has turned cool and crisp, and farm puppy Bo cannot wait to show off his new sweater to all his barnyard friends; however when he finds that the pumpkin patch is a mess he sets out to find just who is responsible. | Identifiers: LCCN 2022009032 (print) | LCCN 2022009033 (ebook) | ISBN 9781665905947 (paperback) | ISBN 9781665905954 (hardcover) | ISBN 9781665905961 (ebook) | Subjects: LCSH: Dogs—Juvenile fiction. | Crows—Juvenile fiction. | Farm life—Juvenile fiction. | Friendship—Juvenile fiction. | Autumn—Juvenile fiction. | Sweaters—Juvenile fiction. | CYAC: Dogs—Fiction. | Animals—Infancy—Fiction. | Crows—Fiction. | Farm life—Fiction. | Friendship—Fiction. | Autumn—Fiction. | Sweaters—Fiction. | Classification: LCC PZ7.1.H54497 Sw 2022 (print) | LCC PZ7.1.H54497 (ebook) | DDC [E]—dc23 |
LC record available at https://lccn.loc.gov/2022009032
LC ebook record available at https://lccn.loc.gov/2022009033

CONTENTS

Fall
Is Here!

The sun glimmered through the clouds as I raced around the barn. There was a fresh, crisp scent in the air. And all the trees were bursting with color.

Out in the barn, Wyatt and Imani, my human brother and sister, were busy sweeping the leaves.

I raced toward them as fast as I could to get a better look. But I got a little too excited and tumbled right into the pile!

Oops! Golden-yellow, orange, and

bright red leaves flew everywhere.

As I ran around in happy circles, the leaves made a loud crunching noise. And the brown ones were the crunchiest.

"Hey, Zonks!" I greeted him as I ran over to the pen. "Look at these colorful leaves! I wonder why they change."

"That's because fall is here! The leaves always change when the wind gets cooler," Zonks explained. "It just makes sense, like pigs and mud."

Zonks was right. Some things just made sense. And that's all that mattered.

When I ran back to where Imani and Wyatt were, they had now started a new pile.

I was so tempted to jump back in. But then I heard Jennica, my human mom, call my name.

"Hey, Bo! Come here, boy!" she yelled. She was holding a pup-sized

sweater with maroon and orange stripes. "Look what I knit for you!"

Was it a present for me? It wasn't even my birthday!

I excitedly ran to the porch and sat down in front of her.

"Good boy! Now lift your feet so I can slide this on."

She pulled the sweater over my body as I lifted my paws one at a time. I couldn't wait to see how I looked. So when she held open the screen door, I dashed inside and ran to the mirror. I turned this way and that as I admired my reflection.

I had never understood why humans loved to wear clothes. Why wear clothes when you have fur? Having thick warm fur is one of the best perks of being a dog. But now it finally made sense: this was the coziest sweater ever!

Pumpkin Patch Trouble

I darted out the front door at the speed of light. I couldn't wait to show off my new sweater that was perfect for this chilly weather. The first friend I ran into was Clucks the hen.

"Hiya, Clucks!" I woofed. "My humans made me a sweater. What do you think?"

"Who needs clothes when you have feathers," Clucks said coolly. "But I have to admit, that sweater *does* look pretty cozy."

Clucks wasn't easy to please, so I knew she meant it. I ran around in a happy circle so she could get a good look.

But on the third lap around, I stopped short when I realized we weren't alone. King and Diva came slinking around the corner. And as always, I could tell they weren't in a good mood.

"Wow, what do you know? Your sweater matches that pile of leaves!" Diva said with a smirk.

"Yeah, I'd watch out if I were you," King added. "You might blend right in and get lost!"

I shook my head and dug my paws into the ground as they walked away, hissing with glee. Those barnyard cats didn't know what they were missing. Jumping into a pile of crunchy leaves was the best!

I wondered who I should show my sweater off to next. And that's when I saw exactly who I wanted to see—my friend Comet the foal!

"Hi there, Comet!" I called. "What perfect timing!"

But as she came closer, I could tell something wasn't right.

"Oh, no, Comet, what's wrong?"

Comet neighed and shook her mane nervously. Zonks and Clucks rushed over as well after hearing her voice.

"Oh, Bo! You have to come with me to the pumpkin patch," she said. "Something's not right!"

So with that, Zonks, Clucks, and I followed our friend across the field.

Every year, my human family grows some of the biggest orange pumpkins you'll ever see. Around this time of year, all of us animals know to stay out of the pumpkin patch. Even King and Diva follow the rules!

So when we got there, I couldn't believe what I saw. Almost all the pumpkins had strange dents, and some of them were completely smashed open!

Is It ... the Pumpkin Ghost?

And it turns out, that wasn't even all of it!

"If you think this is bad, the apple orchard is worse," Comet said.

When we ran over to take a look, we saw that Comet was right. Just like the pumpkin patch, the ground was entirely littered with damaged apples.

"Who on Earth could have done this?" Zonks asked with a pout.

"Maybe it's a big hairy monster?"
I asked. "Something spooky like a
pumpkin ghost?"

"Oh, Bo, that's silly. But this *is* quite
odd," Clucks said.

"What do we do now?" Comet
asked worriedly.

I started pacing back and forth, trying hard to think. After going around in circles, I looked back at my paw prints. And that's when I got an idea: we would retrace our steps and look for clues!

So we trudged back up to the pumpkin patch. But as we neared the opening, both Zonks and Clucks stopped to admire the new corn maze. Dogs like me can't pass by a squirrel without going for a chase. But I didn't know pigs and chickens liked corn mazes!

Darnell, my human dad, had built a secret path through the cornfield. I could tell my friends were tired and feeling down. Lucky for me, I knew the perfect game that would cheer them up!

"Hey, this maze is perfect for hide-and-go-sheep!" I cried, forgetting our original plan. "Want to play?"

My friends perked up as I led the way. But as soon as we drew closer, we saw that a whole row of cornstalks was broken!

"Hey, Bo," Comet whinnied. "We should probably play hide-and-go-sheep another time."

Comet was right. Now was not the time to play. The damage was out of control, and we had a serious Davis farm mystery to solve!

The Pumpkin Patch Culprit

After the short corn maze detour, my friends and I were back on track. We arrived at the pumpkin patch, and it was time to look for clues.

It's a good thing dogs have good noses. I can smell things from a mile away! So I put my head down and started walking along.

Soon I noticed some footprints by a large broken pumpkin. Then when I peeked around it, I spotted a shiny black feather, too!

This feather must belong to the pumpkin patch culprit! I thought.

I studied the footprints but didn't recognize them at all. Zonks saw me digging at them and came over to look at them too.

He looked at the prints for a few seconds until his eyes grew wide.

"Hey, Clucks," he called. "Could the chicks at the coop have wandered over here somehow?"

"They certainly did not!" Clucks clucked loudly. "Thank you very much!"

"Well, it's just that these tracks look like small bird prints, and I thought . . ." Zonks trailed off quietly.

Clucks held her head high and strutted over to where we were standing.

"Look here, I can tell you why it wasn't any of the chicks," Clucks said. "See this feather? It's black! The chicks have yellow feathers, of course."

Zonks and I examined the feather and nodded our heads.

"And these footprints in the dirt are most definitely not a chicken's!"

I stared at Clucks's feet and at the prints in the ground. She was right again! While the culprit's footprints were similar, they weren't the same shape.

I was so glad that we could rule out all the chickens. But that meant we still didn't have any leads. So I grabbed the black feather in my mouth and headed over to the apple orchard. Whoever the culprit was, I knew there were more clues to find.

And sure enough, when we went back to the orchard, we found the same mysterious footprints and more black feathers.

I looked around and chased my tail until I saw something fly by out of the corner of my eye.

I stopped and got low to the ground.
And then suddenly I heard a fluttering
of wings. I spun around quickly, but
the bird was already getting away!

Coco
the Crow

"Hey, wait!" I called out. "Come back!"

But the bird was too fast. I chased it through the forest as fast as I could.

At last, the bird landed on a tree branch, and Zonks, Clucks, Comet, and I finally caught up to it. The bird peered down at us from up in the tree and said, "Why are you following me?"

"Um, hi there. My name is Bo. What's your name?" I asked.

"Coco," the bird replied matter-of-factly.

"I've never seen you around the farm before," I said.

Living on a farm full of all kinds of animals, I've seen my share of birds come by—the robins and blue jays are some of the nicest birds you'll ever meet! Lots of pigeons like to come by the farm too. But I had definitely never seen a bird like Coco before. She had jet-black feathers all over her body.

I looked over at my friends to see if they recognized the black bird. But none of them did.

"Well, I'm a crow, and I don't live on a farm," Coco responded before looking away. Then she ruffled her feathers in a way that reminded me of King and Diva.

I looked hard at her black, glossy feathers. "Um, Coco, have you been coming to the pumpkin patch a lot lately?" I asked, choosing my words carefully.

Right away, Coco puffed up her chest.

"I haven't got the slightest idea what you're asking," she cawed.

But just then, a single black feather drifted down from Coco's perch and landed on the ground at my feet.

I didn't want Coco to fly away, so I stayed quiet. But all my doggy senses were on high alert. If we were going to get this bird to talk, I knew we'd have to get to know her first.

So I grabbed my friends for a game-time huddle. We needed a plan B. Fast.

And that's when Zonks whispered the most perfect question.

"What about finishing that game of hide-and-go-sheep?"

I jumped up and gave my pig pal a high-five. No matter who you are, every animal likes to have fun. So I took a deep breath and gave it a shot.

"Hey, Coco, do you want to play hide-and-go-sheep with us in the pumpkin patch?" I asked.

My friends and I all looked up and waited.

And waited some more.

Until finally Coco nodded and led the way back to the pumpkin patch.

Hide–and–Go–
PEEP!

"Hey, Clucks. You, Zonks, and Comet stay together," I said, breaking us into teams. "I'll play with Coco."

Then Coco and I decided to hide first. And I found the perfect hiding spot right away. In the center of the patch, there was one large pumpkin that was big enough to hide both of us.

I crouched down. The secret to hide-and-go-sheep was to not make a sound. Not even a little peep. But I quickly realized that Coco didn't know the rules!

She flapped her wings, kicked up dirt, and littered seeds all over the place. I couldn't believe it. For such a small bird, she sure was an expert at making a big mess.

I tried to calm her down. But nothing worked. And not only that, but Coco also kept on talking—and oh boy, could she talk *a lot*!

She had so much to say. She wondered why not all animals can fly.

And why pumpkin vines were long and twisty. And then she asked me if I knew why birds sat in trees.

I didn't know what to say. But I had to admit, she had good questions that made me think too.

And one thing was for sure: Coco was a one-of-a-kind bird with a very loud voice. I knew my friends would find us quickly. And just like that, they did!

"Found you!" Zonks oinked as he rounded the corner with the others.

"That was way too easy," Comet said. "We could hear you from all the way over there!"

I came out of our hiding spot with my tail between my legs. This round wasn't our best. But hide-and-go-sheep was one of my favorite games. And I knew it was never too late to turn things around. Maybe Coco would be better at seeking.

After we counted down, Coco and I searched and searched. I sniffed the ground for clues while Coco followed, leaving a trail of pumpkin seeds behind us.

I was sure that
my friends would
have a hard time
hiding. Trying
to hide a horse
wasn't going to
be easy.

But Zonks, Comet, and Clucks were
much better hiders than I thought.
We couldn't find them anywhere!

And I could tell Coco was getting tired. After all that nonstop talking, suddenly she was super quiet.

So finally I let out a loud bark to let my friends know that we had given up.

After hearing my voice, my friends
came out from behind a massive tree
trunk.

Losing is never easy. But I knew my friends had won fair and square.

That's when I looked over at Coco, but she was nowhere to be found. After all that chaos, she had disappeared without a trace!

Telling
the Truth

This time Zonks, Comet, Clucks, and I teamed up to find Coco. We looked in the pumpkin patch and ran over to the orchard, but we couldn't find any clues.

As I paced back and forth, that's when I remembered what Coco had said about birds sitting in trees.

So my friends and I ran to the forest
to the spot where we first met her.

And sure enough, there she was.

"Hey, Coco, are you okay?" I asked.

"What's wrong?"

"Oh, Bo, I didn't mean to be so bad at the game," Coco muttered quietly. "Sometimes when I get excited, I peck and nibble at everything!" She flapped her wings as she let out a little caw. "It happens when I'm nervous, too," she continued. "So the only thing I'm good at is making big messes!"

69

"Oh, Coco, don't feel bad," Comet neighed sweetly.

"Yeah, we're all good at different things," I added.

Zonks oinked and Clucks cooed in agreement.

Coco puffed up her chest as she let out a deep breath.

"I want to believe that," she began. "But I'm the one who's been making a big mess all over the farm."

I could tell Coco had more to say. So I sat up and waited for her to continue.

"I just can't help it!" Coco cried. "When I saw all the new pumpkins and apples, I needed to check them out."

Coco let out a sad caw and
kept her head low.

"None of you would
understand," she went
on. "And there's
no way I can fix
all the damage."

Coco was right. Dogs and crows are definitely different.

But animals know animals best. And we all have our own quirks.

"Coco, we know you didn't mean any harm," I said gently.

"Yeah, Coco. Don't be so sad," Zonks agreed. "No problem is too big to fix on this farm."

Coco let out
a loud caw of
relief and hugged
each of us before flying off for the day.

Now, my friends and I didn't want
Coco to feel too bad. But we weren't
sure what to do anymore. Turns out
that some messes are way too big
for a dog, chicken, horse, and pig to
figure out. Luckily for
us, though, I had a
good puppy dog
feeling my human
family would know
exactly what to do.

Only
One Solution

When I got back to the house, Wyatt and Imani were snuggled on the couch. I was so tempted to hop up and join them under the blanket.

But I knew I had a job to do. So I ran in circles and barked at the top of my lungs. As I ran off with one of Wyatt's socks, I almost bumped into the mirror.

And that's when I saw that my new
sweater was filthy! It was covered in
corn kernels, pumpkin seeds, and a
whole lot of mud.

"Bo, what did you do?" Jennica cried. "You're an absolute mess!"

Wyatt stood up and got ahold of me. Then he pulled the sweater over my head and examined it.

"We need to go check out what's going on at the farm!" he cried. "There are pumpkin seeds all over this!"

So finally my family followed me outside. Clucks, Comet, and Zonks were already there waiting for us at the pumpkin patch.

"Whoa, what in the world has happened here?" Imani asked as she stepped over a broken squash.

As the kids started picking up some broken pumpkin pieces, I jumped up and down to get Darnell's and Jennica's attention. They needed to see the mess at the apple orchard and corn maze, too.

When we got to the orchard, Darnell
picked up a smashed apple.

83

"I'm afraid this is the handiwork of a very curious crow," he said, his face growing serious.

I barked and wagged my tail. Sometimes humans were much smarter than I gave them credit for.

"A crow?" the kids cried as they ran over at top speed.

"Yes, it looks like you're right," Jennica replied. "And there's only one solution for that."

What's a Scarecrow?

"Scarecrow?" I perked up. "What's that?"

Zonks shook his head. "Beats me, Bo! Never heard of that one before."

But just like I'd hoped, it was clear my human family had a plan.

Back at the barn, my friends and I watched as everyone got to work.

Darnell and Wyatt gathered some
of the damaged cornstalks. Then
while Jennica collected some apples,

Imani walked over to the patch, picked the last round pumpkin, and brought it back to the barn.

Imani set her pumpkin on the worktable and carefully drew two black eyes, a nose, and large scary teeth.

Meanwhile Wyatt and Darnell gathered wood and started building something with the cornstalks.

Soon all the barnyard animals had come to watch too. Once Darnell finished making and securing the base, Imani lifted the pumpkin face and put it on top.

Then came the finishing touch. Wyatt grabbed my muddy, stained sweater and put it over the scarecrow's body.

"I've never seen a scarecrow before," Clucks began. "But it sure looks spooky."

"Yeah, maybe scarecrows are supposed to *scare* crows!" Zonks cried. "Get it?"

"What? You mean it's supposed to keep crows *away*?" I asked, worried. "We wanted to help Coco, not keep her away forever!"

Was my plan to ask for help going to be a total flop? Was Coco going to blame us?

I paced back and forth in a panic. Before Coco came back, we had to figure out a way to get rid of it. Fast.

So I ran into it. I dug my paws in
and tugged at it. But it wouldn't budge.
Not even one bit.

And Jennica sure wasn't going to let me get even more dirty. So as she picked me up and started back  toward the house, I barked at my friends to say good-bye and helplessly buried my face into Jennica's arms.

Was this spooky scarecrow going to scare Coco away for good?

Sweater
Weather Fun

For the next several days I waited for Coco. The nights grew colder, and the sun was out for less and less time each day. No matter how long I waited, there was no sign of Coco anywhere.

I also missed my cozy sweater on chilly days like this. I had never meant to make it so dirty.

But when you're a dog, getting messy is part of life.

"Hey, Bo!" Jennica called, my ears perking up.

When I turned around, it was as if she had read my mind. In her hands, Jennica was holding a brand-new sweater. Just for me!

I barked happily, wagging my tail as Jennica slipped the sweater over my head.

I jumped up and licked her nose to say thank you.

This time I was going to take good care of my sweater, no matter what! I yipped happily as she gave me a loving pat on the head.

Then I ran over to the window and scanned the fields one more time. And that's when I saw it. Something tiny and black flew across the clear blue sky.

My doggy senses were telling me to get outside, fast. I dashed out to the fields, and sure enough, it was just the bird I had been hoping to see—Coco!

"Hiya, Bo!" Coco cawed excitedly.

I jumped and ran in happy circles. "Oh, Coco, I'm so glad you came back!" I woofed. "I was worried that the scarecrow might have really scared you away!"

"Scared?" Coco asked. "I saw your sweater from up in the sky and thought it was you!"

"You thought it was me?" I asked, amused.

"Yeah, I was coming over to say hi!" Coco replied happily. "And now I have the perfect place to perch when I visit!"

I was so worried that Coco would be sad. But it turns out this was the perfect solution! Coco now had a place to belong on the farm without getting into trouble. And that's what mattered.

"Thanks for being such a good friend, Bo," Coco cawed sweetly. "It means a lot to have a special place to come see friends."

I let out a happy bark. There was always room for more animals on the Davis farm.

And now that Coco was back for a
visit, I had an idea.

"Hey, Coco, want to play a round of
hide-and-go-sheep?" I asked.

"Oh, I was hoping you'd ask," Coco said. Then she lifted her beak and cawed loudly.

Before we knew it, Zonks, Clucks, and Comet ran over to where we

were. They had been eagerly waiting for Coco to come back too.

Now that we were all back together, it was time to have fun! But without fail, that's when Coco started cawing very, very loudly. Oops!

Well, I guess some things aren't meant to change; Coco will probably always be very bad at hide-and-go-sheep. That's just a fact.

But at least we knew how to handle it this time. Sort of.

As Zonks, Clucks, and Comet were counting down, Coco and I jumped into a big pile of crunchy fall leaves. It was the coziest, comfiest hiding spot ever!

And in that moment, it no longer mattered if we won or lost. Life was good, the fall air was crisp,

118

and it was the perfect day to wear my
new sweater. And maybe get it just a
little bit dirty.

Here's a peek at Bo's next big adventure!

My name is Bo, and you need to know something about me. I love springtime at the Davis farm!

The sweet smell of freshly cut grass, the sun shining overhead, and brand-new flowers everywhere, waiting to be dug up.

An excerpt from *All You Need Is Mud*

But after a spring rain, there's only one place to find me—running through the field.

Why? Because all that grass was covered with tiny drops of water that keep me cool.

So, of course, it all started with a dash through the field. My tongue and ears flapped in the breeze. Everything was perfect. Until I reached the barn.

Two small shadows were waiting in the doorway. It was King and Diva, the barn cats.

"Why does that pup keep running

An excerpt from *All You Need Is Mud*

through the fields making such a racket?" King asked.

"Bo the bumbler *is* such a bother!" Diva agreed. "And the smell of wet puppy is so very yucky."

"I heard even the skunks think he stinks," said King. "Pee-yew!"

In case you don't know, cats and dogs don't always get along. Me and the barn cats, though, well, we almost never got along.

"Sorry, King and Diva," I called out. "You grumps can't get me down today!"

An excerpt from *All You Need Is Mud*